THE FIRST PEOPLE

Volume 2

Rick Steber—Writing

Don Gray—Illustrations

Printed in the West
by
Maverick Publications

ISBN 0-945134-76-2

BONANZA PUBLISHING • PRINEVILLE, OREGON

According to popular theory the discovery of North America was made by wandering Mongoloid people who arrived from Asia between 15,000 and 40,000 years ago.

While the exact time of their arrival is passionately debated by anthropoiogists, many facts surrounding these events are generally accepted. Most scientists believe the migrations took place during the Ice Age. So much moisture was held in the form of ice that the ocean level dropped hundreds of feet and the coastal land strip along the Pacific was many miles wider than today.

Gradually the earth warmed, glaciers began to melt and recede and a land bridge was exposed between Asia and North America where the Aleutian Islands are now located. Small groups of Mongoloid people, probably families, crossed this natural bridge and traveled south toward a warmer climate.

As the glaciers continued to melt, the ocean rose, drowning this plain. Inland, from the coast range to the Rocky Mountains, valleys and basins were covered with water from the receding mountain glaciers. Huge marshes grew lush foliage and were inhabited by many animals which are now extinct.

The people who came to live in this region were big game hunters. They used the domestic dog (brought with them from Asia) to drive animals, including mastodon and mammoth, giant ground sloths, camels, horses and the long-horned bison, into marshy areas where they became mired in the mud.

The hunters attacked with spears, clubs and rocks and the battles between man and beast were vicious and cruel. If the hunting party was successful a great deal of effort, with crude stone tools, was required to butcher the animal. A kill meant food for the people, a warm hide for clothing or shelter and stories of adventure and great courage to tell around the fire.

CLOVIS CULTURE

The elephant hunters are the first well-documented people of North America. They left behind large, beautifully worked blades and projectile points chipped from obsidian. This "Clovis-type" point was first found with fossilized elephant bones near Clovis, New Mexico. Similar spear points have been found with mastodon bones in Sequim, Washington and camel bones at Lower Klamath Lake, Oregon.

In addition to hunting large mammals evidence suggests these primitive people also hunted smaller game, trapping them and digging them from their burrows, robbed bird nests, collected berries and dug roots.

THE CAVE PEOPLE

In 1938 anthropologist Dr. L.S. Cressman and his crew excavated a portion of Fort Rock Cave in central Oregon and made an important discovery linking the cave to a prehistoric tribe of cave dwellers.

They unearthed stone and bone artifacts, scrapers, projectile points, drills and awls, and found a few basket and wood fragments.

Then, buried beneath a layer of powdery volcanic pumice, they came across a cache of 75 sagebrush bark sandals. Carbon-dating established they had been worn by people more than 9,000 years ago.

The excavation continued to bedrock where charcoal samples were taken and tested in a laboratory. The dating of man's first campfire in Fort Rock Cave was set at 13,600 years ago.

ERUPTION OF MT. MAZAMA

About 7,500 years ago Oregon's Mt. Mazama erupted so violently the top third of the mountain, one of the tallest in the Cascade range, was blown away and later filled with the deep blue waters of Crater Lake. The sound of the explosion carried for more than one thousand miles and a great cloud of pumice spewed into the atmosphere. Ash fell as far away as Montana and for months volcanic dust obscured the sun.

Scientists believe this eruption and other factors caused a change in the weather. The climate became hotter and drier as a pattern of warm winds blew from the south. The inland marshes dried and the vast lakes evaporated. Springs abruptly stopped flowing. Tall grasses withered and died. All of the large mammals hunted by the Clovis people became extinct, not only from the climatic change but also, some believe, because of the remarkable skill of the hunters.

In order to survive, the elephant hunters were forced to adapt their tools, weapons and living habits to take advantage of the local resources. They turned their attention to antelope, deer, elk and bighorn sheep that had begun to thrive in the absence of the larger mammals.

Small groups of people went out seeking places where game was plentiful and living conditions most favorable. New areas were occupied. Trade developed between these scattered tribes of people.

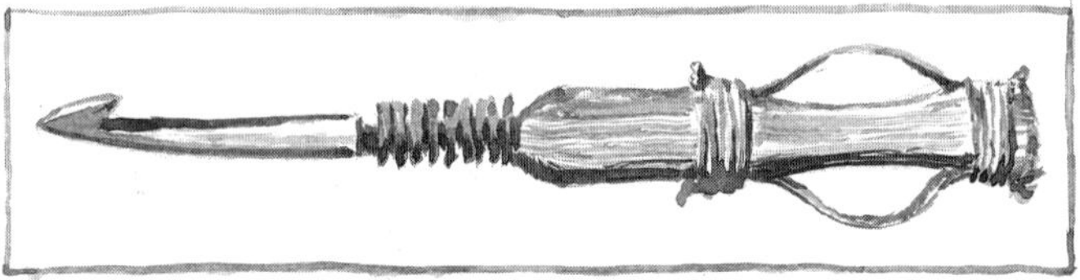

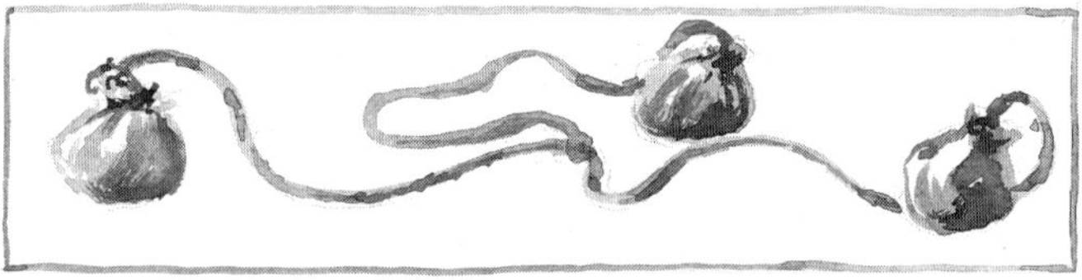

WEAPONS

One of the most important devices ever invented by man was the atlatl, or throwing stick. In principle it was an extension of the arm and added leverage, allowing a spear or dart to be thrown farther and with more power.

Evidence of the use of this ancient device dates back 15,000 years in Europe. One of the oldest atlatl artifacts in the Northwest was uncovered by work crews cutting a road in the

Columbia Gorge in 1960. They unearthed a piece of an atlatl that was dated about 6000 B.C.

Another important discovery from this era was the bola, a rope with weights attached, believed to have been first used in South America. This weapon was thrown so that the weighted ropes wrapped around the prey and brought it down.

The bola was used extensively in the Great Basin along the Pacific Flyway where the native people devised many methods of taking the plentiful waterfowl. One effective method used in the Klamath Basin of southern Oregon was hunting from floating blinds. The hunters used calls carved from bird bones and decoys made of duck skins stuffed with tules to entice ducks and geese to land within reach of their bolas.

BOW AND ARROW

Use of the bow and arrow in Europe dates back at least 6,000 years. But it is believed that the introduction of the bow and arrow to North America was made within the last 3,000 years.

Henry Abbot, a lieutenant in the United States Army attached to the Pacific Railroad Surveys, passed through the Great Basin in 1855. In his writings he described a typical scene:

"The natives are armed with bows and arrows, which they make with great skill. The bows are sticks of soft wood, about three feet in length, backed with deer sinew. The bow string also is of sinew. The arrows are made in three parts. The head is generally of obsidian, which abounds. It is carefully shaped into the usual barbed form, and lashed by deer sinew to one end of a small stick of hard wood about ten inches long. The other end of the stick is inserted into the extremity of a reed and also lashed with sinew. The reed is tipped with feathers, attached by some kind of fastening. This weapon inflicts a dangerous injury...."

Arrow shafts were obtained from any straight-grained, lightweight wood; pine, cedar, willow or yew, or from a bamboo-like cane grass called Phragmites, and even from the stems of cattails.

Not all arrows were tipped with obsidian points. The Modoc Indians, living along the present-day Oregon-California border, used a wooden arrowhead surrounded by a ring of pitch that skipped along the water and into a flock of birds. Other arrows were fitted with bird bone tips because they were lightweight and easily sharpened to a point. In recent times, after contact with the white man, the Northwest Indians began making arrows tipped with a projectile point fashioned from iron or copper.

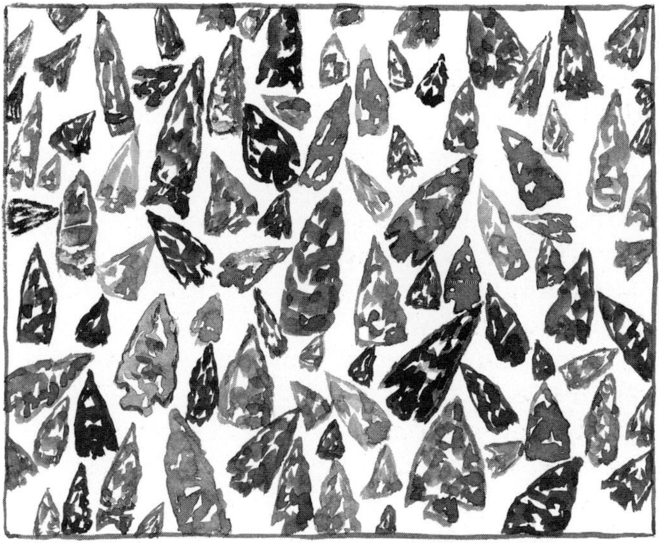

TOOLS OF ARROW MAKING

The tools developed for making an arrow shaft included a knife, a scraper, a straightener and a smoother.

The knife and scraper were most often chipped from obsidian and used for cutting and debarking the shaft. The straightener was made by carving a groove in a rock, heating the rock and inserting the arrow shaft in the groove. Steam generated from moisture in the wood allowed the wood to become malleable and be straightened. The shaft retained this new shape when allowed to cool. Arrow-shaft straighteners, showing evidence of charcoal from being heated in a fire, have been found throughout the Northwest.

Some tribes made do without the straightener and relied instead on a smoother, made from sandstone, pumice, or a similar abrasive stone, to remove any inconsistencies, reduce the shaft to a uniform diameter and polish it.

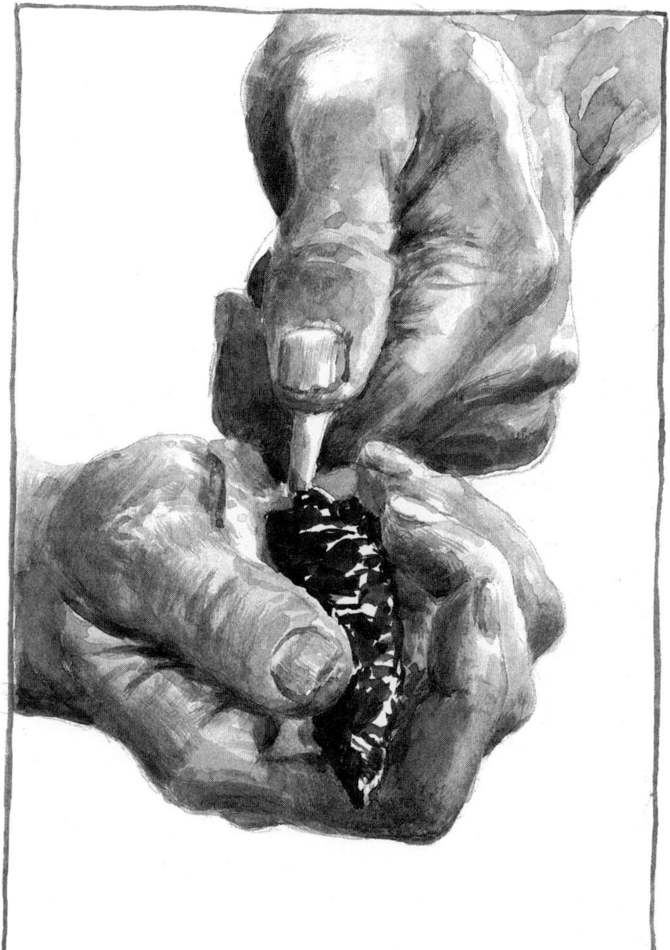

CRAFTING OBSIDIAN

The favorite material for making arrow points was obsidian. It was widely available throughout the Cascade range and across the High Desert, found in outcroppings sometimes hundreds of feet thick where volcanic material flowed to the surface.

Obsidian is a volcanic glass and, except for impurities, very much like ordinary glass. It is usually formed in shades of black, sometimes gray and occasionally with streaks and swirls of red.

Ancient people used a rock to break chunks of obsidian from the flow and carried them back, often many miles, to their village. Pieces of glass suitable for making arrowheads were chipped from the obsidian block by striking a glancing blow with a stone or an antler. If hit correctly thin slivers of obsidian were flaked off.

This same technique, the percussion method, was also used to chip away at the glass and fashion a rough arrowhead. Then the pressure method was used, chipping away flakes of obsidian bit by bit by pressing the pointed end of an antler against the arrowhead. This combination of techniques allowed the craftsman to exercise a great deal of control over the obsidian and, in the hands of a skilled workman, a perfect point could be achieved within a few minutes.

In recent times scientists have discovered a process called "instrumental neutron activation analysis" that allows obsidian to be finger-printed. Each piece of obsidian has certain identifiable trace elements that link it to a specific deposit. Researchers have discovered arrowheads and blocks of obsidian that were carried hundreds of miles from their source.

Another quality of obsidian that makes it valuable to science is that it can be dated. This complex process is based on the knowledge that a slice of obsidian, when exposed to the atmosphere, will absorb water at a given rate. Taking into account a region's climate, the age of an arrowhead can be established by measuring the depth that moisture has penetrated the surface.

SUBSISTENCE

Each region of the Northwest provided the native people with different food sources. The majority of coast dwellers lived in permanent or semi-permanent settlements and ate whatever the sea provided. They gathered mussels, clams and other shellfish and seafood from tidal pools. Some of the North coast tribes were deep-sea fisherman and hunted and killed whales.

They also took food offerings from the land. Women harvested seeds and berries as they ripened. They gathered the wapato, a wild potato that grew along the lower Columbia and other estuaries. Men hunted deer and elk, not only for the meat but also for making buckskin clothing. They killed bears, wolves and smaller animals.

Fish were taken while standing on rocks or platforms built over river rapids. As the migrating salmon and sea-run trout exposed themselves in the fast water they were speared or caught in dip nets. Another successful method of fishing was to build a weir across a tributary stream.

The first people who inhabited the inland region, between the Coast range and the Rocky Mountains, were fortunate in having an abundant supply of large animals. But as the mammoth, bison, horse and camel became scarce, and finally extinct about 7,500 years ago, the people turned to the resources provided by the rivers, marshes, prairies, mountains and the open country of the High Desert. In winter the inland tribes lived in semi-permanent camps but during warm weather months they ranged over the country.

They used dogs to hunt deer and set fires to drive animals. Herds of antelope were driven into natural corrals and killed. Mountain sheep were stalked or shot from blinds. Rabbits as well as other small rodents and birds were trapped with snares and nets. Fish were caught in weirs. Birds were taken with bolas, atlatls and bow and arrows. Women scoured the countryside gathering a variety of seeds, roots, nuts and fruits.

Typical of the people were the Paiute Indians who came to occupy southeastern Oregon and Nevada. They lived in small wandering bands and took food from certain areas. Ownership of the land was not held by a tribe or individual, only the privilege to use the resources was recognized. The names of these bands reveal their food-taking habits: "Crawfish Eaters", "Seed Eaters", "Wild Onion Eaters", "Woodchuck Eaters", "Salmon Eaters" and "Jackrabbit Eaters".

The inhabitants of the Columbia Plateau relied on salmon and sea-run trout that migrated up the Columbia River nine months of the year. At Five-Mile Rapids and Celilo Falls the Indians developed a method of preserving salmon by drying the meat and pounding it into a powder. This established them as traders and allowed the building of permanent villages.

The Lewis and Clark Expedition passed through this area in 1805 and members commented on the number of baskets of dried salmon, about 80 pounds per basket, the Indians had stacked in piles ready for exchange.

Throughout the ages the general division of labor between men and women remained the same. It was the man's domain to protect his tribe and bring in meat. The woman was expected to perform all the other duties: bearing and caring for children, gathering berries and seeds, digging roots and bulbs, drying salmon and game meat, preserving food, tending the fire, preparing food and cooking meals. She cooked over an open fire, or by placing hot stones in baskets of water to heat liquids, or in earthen ovens to bake roots, mussels and other edibles.

SPIRIT WORLD

The first white men to arrive in the Northwest reported the Indians living here believed in ghosts, the supernatural and other worlds. The spirits, both friendly and unfriendly, were always present and their powers had to be dealt with.

The Chinook Indian legend of their creation was a story passed through generations. It told of an old woman and two young girls who came from a place far to the north. They were the only people in all the land. One day the girls sat on a large rock, wishing for husbands so that they might have children and families. A ghost appeared to them and instructed them to look in the other world if they wanted husbands. He made the earth open. The girls saw two men surrounded by fire. This vision scared them, they ran away to the old woman. She too, had seen the vision. That night, while the girls slept, the men of fire came, took them away and they became stars overhead in the heavens. Later the girls allowed their children to come from the sky to earth. They settled along the Columbia River and became the Chinook Indian people.

For many tribes Coyote represented more than an animal. Coyote could be a supernatural being; he could do good or play evil tricks on people and animals of the forest.

Overseeing the spirit world of good and evil was the shaman, or medicine man. He had special powers of enlightenment and could bring good fortune and ward off misfortune, heal the sick, and kill anyone who displeased him. The shaman was both revered and feared. He was one of the wealthiest and most prestigious members of the tribe. But sometimes, if a shaman lost his power and failed to perform magic or heal the sick, he could be required to make amends by forfeiting his life.

COMING OF THE WHITE MAN

Life repeated itself. Centuries passed. For the first people very little ever changed. If changes did occur they happened slowly, over generations, centuries, millenniums.

Then the white man arrived. He carried with him diseases from which the native population had no natural immunities. The white intruders unleased plagues of smallpox, fever, tuberculosis, measles and venereal diseases.

John K. Townsend, who came west with the first missionaries in 1835, wrote of his introduction to the Indians: "The depopulation has been truly fearful. A gentleman told me that only four years ago, as he wandered near what had been formerly a thickly peopled village, he counted no less than sixteen dead men and women, lying unburied and festering in the sun in front of their habitations. Within the houses, all were sick; not one had escaped the contagion; upwards of a hundred individuals, men, women and children, were writhing in agony on the floors with no one to render them any assistance....

"Probably there does not now exist one, where five years ago there were a hundred Indians; and in sailing up the Columbia River, from the cape to the Cascades, the only evidence of the existence of the Indian is an occasional miserable wigwam, with a few wretched half-starved occupants."

In the span of a single generation, after the arrival of the white man, the Indian population of the Northwest, estimated to have been in excess of 100,000, had been reduced to fewer than 15,000. And these survivors, so few in number and spread over such a large territory, could offer little resistance as the pioneers flooded in and took control of the land.

The first people, and their way of life, were gone forever.

Books by Rick Steber

TALES OF THE WILD WEST

A continuing series that celebrates the rich history of the West. Each volume contains 50 short stories. Current titles include: *OREGON TRAIL, PACIFIC COAST, INDIANS, COWBOYS, WOMEN OF THE WEST, CHILDREN'S STORIES, LOGGERS, MOUNTAIN MEN, MINERS, GRANDPA'S STORIES, CAMPFIRE STORIES.*

OREGON TRAIL— LAST OF THE PIONEERS

Our final link to history's most famous trail is the firsthand accounts of these last living pioneers.

HEARTWOOD

Stories of the men and women who settled the West. A treasure you will want to pass on to your children and grandchildren.

NEW YORK TO NOME—THE NORTHWEST PASSAGE BY CANOE

The true adventure of the 1936-1937 expedition to discover the Northwest Passage.

WILD HORSE RIDER

A biography of the 1912 World Saddlebronc Champion, Lew Minor.